Big Babies

by Daniel Jacobs

Consultant: Robyn Barbiers, D.V.M.,
Vice President, Lincoln Park Zoo

Yellow
Umbrella
Books
for early readers

Yellow Umbrella Books are published by Red Brick Learning
7825 Telegraph Road, Bloomington, Minnesota 55438
http://www.redbricklearning.com

Editorial Director: Mary Lindeen
Senior Editor: Hollie J. Endres
Senior Designer: Gene Bentdahl
Photo Researcher: Signature Design
Developer: Raindrop Publishing
Consultant: Robyn Barbiers, General Curator, Lincoln Park Zoo, Chicago, Illinois
Conversion Assistants: Jenny Marks, Laura Manthe

Library of Congress Cataloging-in-Publication Data
Jacobs, Daniel, 1969-
  Big Babies / by Daniel Jacobs
        p. cm.
  Includes index.
  ISBN 0-7368-5827-X (hardcover)
  ISBN 0-7368-5257-3 (softcover)
  1. Mammals—Infancy—Juvenile literature. I. Title. II. Series.
  QL706.2.J33 2005
  599.13'9—dc22

                                        2005015607

Photo Credits:
Cover: Digital Vision Photos; Title Page: Jupiter Images; Page 2: Corbis; Page 3: Jupiter
Images; Page 4: Joe McDonald/Corbis; Page 5: Brand X Pictures; Page 6: Corbis; Page 7:
Digital Vision Photos; Page 8: Galen Rowell/Corbis; Page 9: Corbis; Page 10: Michael
DeYoung/Corbis; Page 11: Image State Photos; Page 12 and 13: (www.OceanLight.com)
Phillip Colla; Page 14: The Image Bank

1 2 3 4 5 6 11 10 09 08 07 06

Table of Contents

Oh Baby!.................................2

Giraffes 4

Elephants 6

Caribou 8

Hippos.................................10

Whales.................................12

Big, Bigger, Biggest! 14

Glossary 15

Index..................................16

Oh Baby!

Most animal babies need special care. They need to be fed. They need to be kept safe. Animal babies need to learn how to do new things. This kitten is cute, cuddly, and little. Not all animal babies are this small!

These tiger **cubs** may look cute, but they are big! Other animal babies can be even bigger. What are these babies like? Get ready to see them and find out!

Giraffes

Thud! A baby giraffe drops a long way to the ground when it is born. The fall does not hurt. The baby soon stands up. Its legs are very long! A newborn giraffe **calf** is taller than most human grown-ups.

A new calf drinks milk from its mother. As the giraffe gets older, it learns to use its long, strong tongue. Then the calf is ready to eat leaves, just like the bigger giraffes.

Elephants

Step, step, step! One of the first things a
baby elephant learns is how to walk. The
baby elephant's mother gently pushes her
baby under her. The mother helps her calf
match its steps to hers. This protects the
baby from the hot sun and hungry lions.

These big babies must also learn how to use their **trunks**. Elephants use their trunks to suck up water and spray it! The elephant baby uses its trunk to touch things, move things, and sniff things, too.

Caribou

Clip, clop. Clip, clop! Caribou are big animals that move fast. A caribou calf can run just 90 minutes after it is born. It has to! The caribou's mom and the rest of the **herd** keep moving to find food and to stay safe. The calf has to move, too.

A caribou calf grows very fast. A calf doubles its weight by the time it is about 10 days old. The calf's antlers grow, too. By the time a calf is all grown up, its antlers may be bigger than you are!

Hippos

Splash! A baby hippopotamus is born underwater. The first thing a baby hippo learns to do is swim. It swims to the top of the water to take its first breath. Like older hippos, the baby will spend most of its life in the water. Sometimes, the baby rides on its mother's back.

Soon this baby will follow its mom even when she goes on land. Then the baby hippo will learn which plants are good to eat. When it opens its mouth wide, this big baby will scare other animals away!

Whales

Whoosh! This blue whale is the biggest baby in the world. As soon as it's born, its mother gently pushes it up, up, up! Whales never leave the water, but they need to breathe air. They breathe through holes on the tops of their heads called **blowholes**.

The whale calf's first food is its mother's milk. It gulps down enough milk to gain about 200 pounds (91 kilograms) each day! These big babies also take long, long trips. They follow their moms and swim thousands of miles (kilometers) across the ocean.

Big, Bigger, Biggest !

Animal babies keep growing. It takes years for these babies to grow up. As they get bigger, they learn more. When they are fully grown, they will be ready to have babies of their own.

Glossary

blowhole—a breathing hole on the top of the head of a whale or dolphin

calf—a large baby animal such as an elephant, giraffe, caribou, or whale

cub—a baby animal such as a tiger, lion, bear, or wolf

herd—a group of animals of the same kind that live and travel together

trunk—an elephant's long nose that can be used to lift things and suck up water

Index

antlers, 9
blowhole, 12
blue whale, 12
breathe, 12
calf, 4, 5, 6, 8, 9
caribou, 8, 9
cubs, 3
elephant, 6, 7
giraffe, 4, 5, 14
herd, 8
hippo, 10, 11

kitten, 2
learn, 6, 7, 10, 11, 14
milk, 5, 13
plants, 11
run, 8
swim, 10, 13
tiger, 3
tongue, 5
trunks, 7
walk, 6
whale, 12, 13

Word Count: 535
Early-Intervention Level: M